The Devil Made Me Do It

DONALD RAY GOODMAN

short stories

The Devil Made Me Do It

DONALD RAY GOODMAN

short stories

iUniverse, Inc.
Bloomington

The Devil Made Me Do It

iUniverse books may be ordered through booksellers or by contacting:

iUniverse
1663 Liberty Drive
Bloomington, IN 47403
www.iuniverse.com
1-800-Authors (1-800-288-4677)

Because of the dynamic nature of the Internet, any Web addresses or links contained in this book may have changed since publication and may no longer be valid. The views expressed in this work are solely those of the author and do not necessarily reflect the views of the publisher, and the publisher hereby disclaims any responsibility for them.

ISBN: 978-1-4759-6106-5 (sc)
ISBN: 978-1-4759-6107-2 (e)

Library of Congress Control Number: 2012921078

Printed in the United States of America

iUniverse rev. date: 1/17/2013

Dedication

To my friend William (Bud) Pavey, may he rest in peace.

To my friend Robert (Mitzu) Stanton, may he rest in peace.

To my parents, Thurman and Helen Goodman,
may they rest in peace.

Table of Contents

Foreword

My father, Donald Goodman, has always been a storyteller. When I was seven, Dad began driving me twice a week to judo practice; these trips from Spencer, Indiana, to Bloomington continued until I was fourteen. We would drive through the old neighborhood where my father grew up, and over the years, Dad was never short of a story from his past.

Although he was an avid reader, it was a bit of surprise to me that my father undertook the project of writing down some of these stories. It all began last Christmas, when my sister, Dawn, enrolled him in a writing class; from that point on, Dad began keeping a scrapbook. My wife is a graphic designer for Author Solutions, and for Dad's seventy-third birthday, we presented him with a publishing package. Authors often begin with the dream of writing a book or publishing a collection; my father is just a storyteller, with a fond memory for shenanigans, who just happened to be obliged by the gifts of a writing class and a publishing package.

The Devil Made Me Do It is a collection of biographical anecdotes that highlight mostly humorous moments from Dad's life. It is not a book written for the masses; in fact, my father originally intended to only distribute copies of his scrapbook to friends and family—those who might intimately relate to the stories. Other readers will appreciate the collection if they have a taste for honest humor and mostly benign real-life mischief.

The Devil Made Me Do It will also appeal to local historians and folklorists of the Hoosier state, and particularly of Monroe and Owen Counties, with its personal narratives that offer a glimpse into the life and times of the region through the eyes of a native. The collection may also appeal to those studying Americana, particularly during the fifties, sixties, and seventies. My father is very much a product of the 1950s, with his unwavering appreciation for fast chrome-lined cars with elegant tail fins, the music of Buddy Holly, and the glory of America and all her conventions. When it comes down to it, *The Devil Made Me Do It* is an account of discovery, growing up, and life experiments—which all too often don't go as planned—in Hoosier Americana.

—Kevin Goodman

Acknowledgments

To Dawn (Sue) Goodman, for enrolling me in the creative-writing class that began this project;

Meera Ray Benton, for her time transcribing my handwritten stories;

Kimberly Benton, for helping transcribe some of my stories;

Luiza Kleina, for designing both the cover and the layout of this book;

Kevin Goodman, for writing the foreword;

Luiza and Kevin, for publishing this book with iUniverse;

and my family, wife, and all the friends who made these stories possible,

thank you.

My Mother Was a Psychic Who Foretold the Future

WHEN I WAS about nine years old, I asked my mother if I could have a bike. I said, "All my friends have bikes."

SHE SAID, "No," and when I asked why not, she said, "Because you will have a wreck and break your arm."

So I went around the corner to Steve Minnick's house to ride his bike. What happened? I had a wreck and broke my arm.

The only other time I ever broke a bone was when I was about four years old. I tied a towel around my neck, climbed on top of a chicken coop in the backyard, announced that I was Superman, and said that I could fly!

Well, I wasn't, and I couldn't. I broke my right wrist. My mother hadn't predicted this accident; I guess she hadn't developed her psychic powers yet.

Circa 1962. My mother holding Marcy and one of her
many pet dogs. Marcy is my sister Nancy's firstborn.

Who Needs Enemies When You Have a Brother Like Me?

ONE SUMMER DAY when I was ten years old, I was complaining, as usual, to my mother that there was nothing to do. She suggested that I take Nancy outside and play a game with my sister. Since Nancy was only five years old, I was the "brains" of the outfit, and it was up to me to think up a game.

We usually played cowboys and Indians, but my mother had confiscated my BB gun, so that wasn't fun anymore.

"I know something we can do," I said. "I saw this in a movie: this man in fancy clothes had this pretty girl stand in front of a wooden wall; he threw knives at her, forming an outline around her body." I told Nancy all she had to do was to stand against the woodshed, and I would do the rest.

I went into the house to get some knives, but then I remembered that my mother had hidden all the knives from me, so I couldn't find any. Good thing I had a backup plan: I would use my brother's archery set. He had a bow with target arrows that had round metal points on the tips that would go through a paper target and stick in a bale of hay. I snuck the bow and arrows outside.

Fortunately for Nancy, I could not pull the bowstring back

very far, so when the arrow hit her in the leg, it only bounced off (after breaking the skin a tiny bit). However, my mother thought this was a big deal and took Nancy to the doctor for a tetanus shot.

Later that summer, the family went fishing down at Twin Lakes. As I tried to cast my line into the water, it hooked onto something and I pulled hard; the screaming and crying told me it was my sister. We took another trip to the doctor to remove the fishing hook from her ear.

To recap, I was now banned from playing with my BB gun, banned from playing with knives, banned from playing with the archery set, and banned from fishing within forty yards of another family member.

Fortunately, I still had my slingshot under the bed.

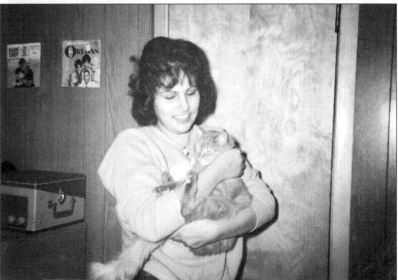

Nancy not only survived her years as my kid sister but blossomed into a pretty teenager and woman, as pictured here.

Not Poor, Just Less Fortunate

PLAYING KICK THE can was one of the favorite games in our neighborhood. Usually there was me, Steve Minnick, Jerry Zink, Billy Lavender, and Alan Freeman. Sometimes Jerry's sisters Roseanne and Joannie Benevole, who lived in the nice brick house on the corner, would join in.

One day we were all playing when Joannie said she had to go home and help her dad. She said he was preparing baskets of fruit to deliver to poor families. Mr. Benevole owned a Mercury dealership in Bloomington, so he could afford things like that.

Later on that evening, there was a knock on the door, and when I opened it, there stood Joannie, holding a basket of fruit.

I was embarrassed but thanked her. Now I never thought that we were poor; we never went hungry or did without anything we really needed. Dad was a housepainter, so he didn't have much work in winter months, and the house we rented was said to have started out as a chicken coop. It had only one door and was heated by two potbelly stoves that burned coal. My brother Bob ran a water pipe into the house, so we did have water inside, but it was not heated. We also didn't own a car. If we wanted to go to town, we walked two miles. (If we cut through the farm fields, it was about one and a half miles.)

Now this sounds like a poverty-level existence, but it was not, for that period in time. World War II had only been over for about three years. No new houses had been built or new cars produced during the war. So a lot of people lived in substandard housing, because that was what was mostly available during the war, and very few used cars were available because new cars were not being mass-produced yet. Most car factories were still retooling from making tanks.

I don't think we were worse off than most of our neighbors; not everyone had indoor plumbing yet, but almost every family had an old car to drive.

The next day, I felt better when most of my friends reported getting fruit baskets too. I would like to think that Joannie's dad had said that he wanted to do something for the families who were less fortunate, not for the families who were poor.

The Awkward Picnic

IN THE SUMMER of 1950, when I was eleven years old, Dad bought our first family car: a 1938 Oldsmobile. To celebrate the occasion, we went on a family picnic.

It was a rare treat for Nancy and me; our older brothers, Bob and Jim, stayed home. They had other things to do.

Mother packed a basket with sandwiches, desserts, and drinks. She also put eating utensils in the basket. When Dad asked her if she had everything we needed, she said we should stop at Vibbart's for some napkins. Mr. Vibbart operated a very small grocery store about two blocks from our house. When we got to the store, Mother sent me in with instructions to buy napkins.

"Hi, Mr. Vibbart," I said. "Mother sent me in to buy napkins."

Mr. Vibbart paused for a second and asked, "Does she want sanitary napkins?"

Well, my eleven-year-old-boy brain processed this question and came to the conclusion that she wouldn't want unsanitary napkins, so I said, "Sure, sanitary napkins."

My Vibbart looked on the shelf and asked, "Does she want a box of regular napkins?" Again my eleven-year-old brain thought that she would not want irregular napkins, so I said, "Sure, regular ones."

So with my purchase in a grocery bag, we drove on to our picnic. When we arrived at our table, mother unpacked the food and utensils. The last thing she did was dump the grocery bag with my purchase on the table. Out rolled a box of Kotex regular pads.

Remember, this was 1950; not only was I an eleven-year-old boy, but in those days, there was no saturation of TV ads extolling the virtues of feminine hygiene products.

How the Boy Scouts Gave Me a Passion for Indiana Basketball— and Were Sort of Responsible for Me Learning to Kiss Girls

I TOOK TO scouting like a duck takes to water. I started off in the Cub Scouts (for ages eight to ten) and then became a Boy Scout (for ages ten to fourteen). Eventually I became an Explorer Scout (for older teens). The Boy Scouts offered camping, hiking, and troop projects; you could also learn valuable skills and earn merit badges on a wide range of subjects.

I belonged to Troop 4, which was one of the bigger troops in Bloomington. There were about sixty members, and our meetings were held in the basement of the Methodist church on Fourth Street. We met every Tuesday night.

I excelled at scouting. I was the leader of Wolf Patrol, which consisted of twelve other scouts.

Eventually, I qualified as a Star Scout, which was two levels below Eagle Scout. The scoutmaster put me in charge of a storeroom full of camping equipment. Anybody who wanted to use the camping gear needed me to sign it out to him.

Spike Dixon was our troop's assistant scoutmaster. He was also the trainer for the Indiana University basketball team. It was his idea to use our troop as ushers to seat people at IU basketball games. While doing this, I developed my love for IU basketball.

In 1953, IU won the Big Ten title; Spike said he would get a team photograph and have all the players sign it. He said we would have some kind of contest and award it to the winner.

The contest was to see who could do the most good deeds in one month. This was one contest I was determined to win ... and I did.

In the meantime, Indiana went on to win the 1953 NCAA tournament, making the autographed picture even more valuable. I still have it.

Explaining how the Boy Scouts were indirectly responsible for me learning to kiss girls is a little more difficult.

When I turned fourteen, I became an Explorer Scout; another Explorer lived across the street from the Methodist Church, where we had our scout meetings. His name was Robin McNeil, and he had a twin sister named Rosie.

Their parents were divorced (rare in the 1950s). They lived with their mother, who was a professor at IU.

I would go to Robin's house to work on Scout projects. Rosie would usually hang around with us. Sometimes the three of us would walk uptown and have an ice cream at the drugstore.

Their mother thought it would be cute if I became Rosie's "boyfriend." One weekend, she drove us to Cascades Park, where we had a picnic and played games. The next Saturday, Rosie invited me to listen to records and play board games at her friend Sandy's house.

Sandy lived on East First Street, four doors down from Dr. Alfred Kinsey (of the infamous sex survey). Her parents had converted an unattached garage into an apartment room for her.

They had card tables, chairs, a record player, records, board games, and a refrigerator filled with sodas.

When Rosie and I arrived, there were two other girls whom Sandy also invited. One of the girls was Linda Hollingsworth, one of the best-looking girls in school.

We started out playing Monopoly. After a while, Sandy said Monopoly was boring and proposed we play another game: spin the bottle!

Oh my God! I thought, *there is only me and four girls. I have died and gone to heaven.* I had never kissed a girl before, but I was eager to try. It was a lot of fun, even though Rosie (who was two inches taller than I was) made me stand on a Coke case to kiss her.

These get-togethers lasted the rest of the summer; different girls sometimes attended, and occasionally there was another boy there.

When I told my friends in the neighborhood that I had kissed several girls at this party, they were jealous. When I told them one of the girls happened to be Linda Hollingsworth, I think I achieved rock-star status.

Those times spent at Sandy's house saved me from being awkward and shy around girls in high school. I could have been afraid to talk to girls, as I was not very tall, and worst of all, my eyes were slightly crossed—not exactly the type to attract girls.

But I had developed a good deal of confidence, despite my physical shortcomings. Thank God Sandy got bored with Monopoly.

I was born with esotropia, a condition that causes one eye to turn inward. My parents opted for corrective glasses to solve the problem. That didn't work, so I was always self-conscious throughout my school years.

When I turned twenty-one, I had surgery on my left eye by realigning a muscle. The doctor said the degree of change in the deviation was reduced from seven degrees to two degrees (the "normal" range).

The photo of IU's 1953 NCAA national champions,
autographed by all the players. I won this for doing the
most good deeds of all the scouts in Troup 4.

Be Careful What You Wish For

My mother liked all kinds of animals as pets. However, for as long as I could remember, she always wanted a monkey. One day I saw an ad in a magazine where you could order one for $19.95, so I did.

After picking it up at the freight station (no UPS back then), I bought a small cage and brought it home. The only problem was that Mother was scared to death of it, even though it looked like an organ grinder's monkey. It was fun to play with.

I would tie the end of his leash to the bottom of a chair, and Mother would cautiously hold out a piece of food until the monkey could just reach it. One time he broke his leash and pounced on the food, which was still in her hand. She let out a scream and did a backward flip on the carpet.

After that evening, I knew one thing for sure: the monkey would not be around much longer. Mother probably wanted to trade it for something else that she had wanted all of her life, like a harp or a polo mallet.

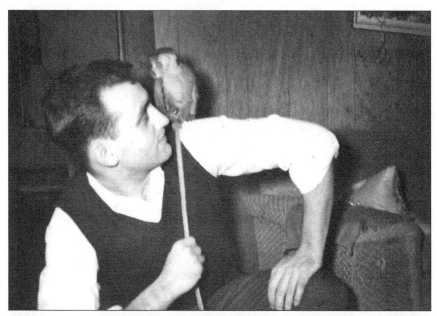

This is the beast that terrified my mother.

How I Got in Trouble for Getting an A+ on My Report Card

I WENT TO Bloomington High School; in 1958, we would carry our report cards from class to class to have each teacher record our grades. Mine was almost completely filled with the letter *C*, meaning average, with one glaring exception. Mr. Van Horn had given me an A+ in psychology. This stood out like a sore thumb.

I had only taken psychology to fill out my curriculum. To my surprise, I found the course both interesting and easy. Because I found the subject interesting, I studied hard, made all As on the tests, and led the way in classroom discussions. Another reason I did so well was because, unlike math or chemistry, which had absolute answers, psychology was more of an abstract study.

I was shocked to learn that other students found the course difficult. Even some of the so-called "brains" were getting lower grades than they usually did in class.

Because some students were struggling with the course, Mr. Van Horn said we could do a paper for extra credit. I already had an A in the class, but I had a project in mind that I wanted to do. I interviewed ten different people on their occupations to find out what kind of problems each occupation posed on their mental health. I got an A+ on my report.

My next class was English, taught by Mrs. Gladys Smith, a "no-nonsense" type teacher. I remember thinking how surprised she would be when she saw that A+. *Surprised* wasn't the word; *disbelieving* was. She told me to take the questionable card upstairs to Mr. Stewart, the assistant principal, so I walked to his office.

I went up to Mr. Stewart's office.

"Don, to what do I owe the pleasure of your visit today?" I guess after four years of high school, we were now on a first-name basis.

I said, "Mrs. Smith doubts the grade I got in psychology."

Mr. Stewart looked at the report card and chuckled. "This is easy to settle," he said. "Let's go down the hall and talk to Mr. Van Horn." Mr. Stewart asked Mr. Van Horn if I had earned an A+ in his class.

Mr. Van Horn confirmed that the grade was authentic. Mr. Stewart asked him if he would write a note to that effect, so I could take it back to Mrs. Smith.

I presented the note and my report card to Mrs. Smith. I was grinning from ear to ear in anticipation of her apology. She read the note (twice, I think), shook her head, and with a sigh recorded my grade for her class on my report card. It was my usual C.

Please Tell Me That Is Not Your Car

When I was a sophomore in high school, I had a good friend named Charlie. One day at school, Charlie said he had saved enough money to buy a car. After school, he took me to his house so I could see it.

It wasn't much of a car, although Charlie was proud of it. It was a 1946 Crosley station wagon. It had two big air horns on the roof and was covered with cartoons, which concealed the rust and dents on the body. It looked like a clown car that had escaped from the circus.

Charlie was sixteen years old and needed to get his driver's license. You had to have a licensed driver with you to take the test. Charlie's mom didn't drive, and I had gotten my license three months earlier, so I went with him to the BMV. I helped him study for the written exam, but he was worried about the driving test.

When I had taken the test, I had to drive around the courthouse a couple of times and then parallel park. Then I had to drive north on Highway 37 to Cascades Park and then return to the BMV.

I told Charlie that parking was not going to be a problem, as his car was only about eight feet long. When the examiner stepped outside and saw Charlie's car, he said, "Please tell me that isn't your car."

"Sure is," Charlie replied. "Can you believe I only paid forty-five dollars for it?"

The examiner took his clipboard and walked very slowly to the Crosley. He walked to the front of the car and had Charlie turn on his lights. Then he walked to the back and asked Charlie to tap his horn. I guess he hadn't noticed how big those air horns were, because he nearly jumped out of his skin when he heard them.

The examiner got into the car and told Charlie to back up. After barely going five feet, the examiner said, "Stop; now move forward!" Again, after moving five feet, the examiner said, "Stop," and then he handed Charlie some papers from his clipboard and said, "Congratulations, you passed."

This is a photo of a 1948 Crosley. This car is a limousine compared to the one Charlie drove: stick two huge air horns on top, then add cartoon characters, rust spots, and dents, and then you would have the car Charlie bought for forty-five dollars.

How I Owned the Car of My Dreams—for One Hour

THE YEAR 1955 was a great year for cars. In May of that year, I got my driver's license and my interest in cars went off the charts. The whole car industry was turning out new cars with style and power. Not just one company, but all of them. And Ford had a brand-new car model: the Thunderbird.

The T-Bird was beautiful, but as a two-seater, it was impractical. You could only take one person with you. In 1958, Ford built a bigger T-Bird that seated four people. That became my dream car.

In 1960, I was working at a factory and putting in a lot of overtime. So I started saving my money in case I saw a used T-Bird for sale. One day, I looked in the *Indianapolis Star* and saw an ad for a car lot that was operated by a shady character who called himself the Used Car King. (He later served time for tax evasion.) He had a 1958 T-Bird for sale.

I had a really nice 1955 Ford Crown Victoria but wanted my dream car. I fell in love with the car the moment I saw it. So I traded in my nice Crown Vic and drove the 1958 T-Bird off the lot.

On the way home, I stopped at a gas station to buy a soda before heading back to Bloomington. At the gas station, I pulled the hood up to check the oil level. I noticed the huge air cleaner on top of the four-barrel carburetor; I thought that if I removed the air cleaner, I could hear that four-barrel roar when I stomped on the gas.

So I took the air cleaner off and put it in the trunk. I got back onto the highway and headed home. When I gave it the gas, the car went *"Varoom, Varoom."* I slowed down and floored it again. This time it went *"Var-clunk, clunk,"* and stopped dead in the road. I put it in neutral and coasted off the highway.

I raised the hood to take a look at the engine; a hose in front of the carburetor had ruptured and antifreeze was sucked into the engine, locking it up. I caught a ride back to the gas station and called the car lot, telling them that the car had stopped running for no reason. They sent a wrecker to tow it in, and I called my friend, Gary, to come and give me a ride home.

Fortunately, the car had a thirty-day 100 percent warranty. I went back to see the manager, and he said the engine had blown. It might take several weeks to find a replacement.

"Well," I said, "let me have my old car back."

"Can't," he said. "We sold it."

We made a deal for the same money on a 1958 gold-and-white Ford Fairlane two-door hardtop. It was nice and had the same big engine as the T-Bird, but it wasn't my dream car.

I am leaning on my 1958 Ford; this is the car I bought when they
said they couldn't fix my "dream car," the 1958 Thunderbird.

I didn't have my T-Bird long enough to take a picture of it,
but it looked like these two. It was white with turquoise, and
white leather interior, like the convertible. Beautiful car!

Harmony in the Workplace

MY FIRST FULL-TIME job after high school was working at the Sarkes Tarzian factory. At the peak of the plant's production, they employed almost three thousand people.

I liked working at Sarkes Tarzian. I worked in what was called "the stick room" with three other guys. We operated machines that fed plastic sticks into a die and dropped small metal contacts into the sticks. These sticks were the main components of TV tuners that were assembled on the production floor.

The machines usually worked with no problem; usually, all we had to do was fill the two bowls that fed sticks and contacts in the machine. Every so often a stick would not seat properly, and we would shut down the machine and fix the problem. (This required hitting a flat-head screwdriver with a ball-peen hammer; it usually only took about five minutes to get the machine running again.)

We had a production quota, which we purposely kept down, fearing if we met the quota, management would raise it, requiring us to work harder.

One day, we got in a new machine, along with a new worker hired to operate it. His name was Junior, and he was straight off the farm in Patricksburg, Indiana.

He didn't go along with our minimum quota, as he wanted

to look good for the boss. I slowed him down every chance I got. He was over six feet tall and weighed 230 pounds; I was five foot nine and weighed 150 pounds.

One day his machine jammed, and while he was trying to fix it, I threw some contacts at his head to distract him. He grumbled and cussed and told me to stop. And I should have, but I didn't. All at once, he whirled around and threw his hammer at my head. I ducked, and the hammer went through a glass window facing the production floor. It sounded like a bomb went off and showered glass all over the floor.

I was sure we would all be fired when the plant manager showed up, but Junior turned out to be a good liar. He told the manager he had forgotten to remove the hammer from the turntable, and when he restarted the machine, the powerful press shot the hammer into the window.

Although the plant manager seemed to buy this explanation, he said he was going to keep his eye on us. So much for harmony in the workplace.

The Wreck of the Hesperus

IN THE EARLY 1960s, the hippie movement had reached IU. Several coffeehouses had popped up around Bloomington. Gary and I decided to visit one, called the Wreck of the Hesperus.

"The Wreck of the Hesperus" was a poem penned in 1842 by Henry W. Longfellow. It told a tale of a sea captain taking his young daughter to sea with him. A storm hit the schooner, and it was so bad, the captain tied his daughter to the mast to keep her from being washed overboard. Later the mast with the dead girl washed ashore as the only remains of the lost ship.

The coffeehouse looked like a wrecked ship, inside and out. You had to climb a boarding plank to enter. Once inside, girls with flowers in their hair served espresso.

For entertainment, people would stand up and read poetry. Instead of applauding, customers would snap their fingers in unison if they liked it.

The espresso coffee was bitter and the entertainment was horrible, so we left, vowing not to become hippies.

This is an artist's conception of the captain of
the Hesperus and his young daughter.

It was a strange name for a coffeehouse.

Who You Gonna Call? Ghostbusters!

Bud Pavey, Gary Gross, Robert Stanton, and I were good friends who hung out together after we all graduated high school.

In the summer of 1958, we often met up at Joe's Roller Rink. Bud and Gary were not much for skating, so we usually went somewhere else for fun. We were always playing jokes on each other, but one day, Bud, Robert, and I decided to play a big one on Gary.

Bud noticed an abandoned house out in the country. He said if we parked at the bottom of the hill and looked up at the house, it would look much more imposing. So we put together a plan to get Gary: Bud would hide in the house and make "ghost" noises as Robert and I led Gary through the house.

That night, Gary joined Robert and me at Joe's Roller Rink; we told him we had heard of a haunted house that we wanted to investigate. Gary had to be convinced; he was very reluctant to go. Eventually, we talked him into it.

We parked at the bottom of the hill and started walking toward the house. It looked somewhat like the house in the movie *Psycho*.

As we got closer to the house, Gary began to get cold feet; he didn't want to climb the fence and go into the pasture surrounding

31

the house, but with Robert on one side and me on the other, we pulled Gary on.

About halfway to the house, we heard, "Snort, snort," and we all froze in our tracks. Robert and I looked at each other; we knew it couldn't be Bud.

I turned my flashlight toward the sound. There in the pasture was a big bull, and he was giving us the evil eye.

I dropped the light and ran for the fence. Gary and Robert not only beat me to the fence, they had already cleared it and were on the other side.

Needless to say, nothing in that house could scare us as much as we scared ourselves in that cow pasture.

"Little" Robert Stanton and Gary Gross at out house in Adel. They were goofing around on my riding mower.

Sadly, Robert and Bud have passed away. Of four
close friends, only Gary and I remain.

Am I Going Too Fast?

IN 1963 MY friend Buy Pavey bought a new car. Not just an ordinary new car, but a fire-engine red Pontiac Bonneville convertible, with white leather interior. It was powered by a 383 cid motor with 3 two-barrel carburetors that produced 340 HP. Man, what a machine! Bud drove the car over to my house, to show it off. After begging Bud to let me drive it, I was allowed to go around the block, at a safe 30mph. Later, I would have my chance to do a lot better than that.

Bud Pavey and Gary Gross were very good bowlers; both of them had won the Bloomington Men's League championship trophy. I, on the other hand, was a rotten bowler. Late one Friday night, Bud and Gary decided to go to Chicago to a bowling tournament, to be held at 10:00AM the next day.

In order to get some rest on the trip, Bud let me drive the Bonneville, because I wasn't going to bowl. Gary stretched out in the back and Bud leaned against the passenger door to catch a nap. After about an hour going north on SR231 I got a good long stretch of road, and I was sure Bud was asleep, I opened the Bonneville up a little.

I was doing about 110mph, according to the speedometer, when I bottomed out a little crossing a rough bridge. That brought

Bed out of his slumber. He let out a scream when he saw that the telephone poles were flying by at an alarming rage.

"What?" I asked, "Am I going too fast?"

"STOP THE CAR!" Bud screamed again. "I will drive the rest of the way!"

That was the last time I got to drive the Bonneville.

Bud Pavey was best man at my wedding at Patricksburg in 1969

Gary Gets Confused

GARY GROSS AND I were always getting into crazy situations. One night, we were riding around in Gary's old Mercury when a fire truck sped by with red lights flashing and its siren blaring. Gross said, "Let's follow it and see where the fire is."

I SAID, "No, Gross, it is against the law to follow a fire truck."

Despite my advice, off we went, right behind the fire truck. It wasn't long before more red lights flashed and sirens blared behind us. I said, "Gross, it's the police; you better pull over."

He said, "Naw, they are just going to the fire."

Just then, the police car pulled alongside us and motioned us over. Gary got the message and stopped the car, and the policeman pulled up behind us. The cop told us to get out of the car. He asked Gary why he hadn't pulled over sooner. Gary said that with all the sirens ahead of him and behind him, he had gotten confused.

The officer asked Gary for his name; he said, "Gary Gross."

"What?" said the cop. "Put your hands on the car and spread your legs."

I thought that was funny and started laughing. The cop said, "You too, buddy." So I stopped laughing and assumed the position. After checking Gary's driver's license, the officer explained that he had thought Gary said, "Gary Groh," who was currently being sought by the police.

We were released with a warning not to follow any more fire trucks.

Gary next to his 1954 Dodge; it was a nice-looking car back then.

What Could Possibly Go Wrong?

ONE DAY GARY called and said to come over and see the new toy he had recently purchased.

It turned out to be a moped. A moped is basically a bicycle with a small gas motor capable of propelling it to speeds of about thirty-five miles per hour.

He told me it was a lot of fun to ride around the neighborhood. Too bad it couldn't carry a passenger so that we both could ride.

"Wait a minute," I said. "I have a great idea. Get me some rope, and I will tie one end of the rope to the back of the moped and one end to the handlebars of Jeff's bike. You could tow me behind you through the neighborhood. What could possibly go wrong?" (You'd think by this time I would stop asking that question.)

We shot down the street for about four blocks before we had to make a turn. When Gary turned, the bike tipped over, dragging me along on my side.

I started yelling for Gary to stop, but he was looking at yard sales and flower beds and continued dragging me on my side through the neighborhood.

Finally, he stopped to see what all the screaming was about. Jeff's bike and I had suffered some injuries. For the bike, it was some scratched paint; for me, I lost some skin off my elbow.

Fortunately, Marylin (Gary's wife) always kept a first-aid kit handy for my visits.

The top photo shows a moped. It looks like a "sissy" form of transportation, but in the wrong hands, it could become a weapon of mass destruction.

In the bottom photo, Gary is driving my lawnmower and I am riding on the handlebars. I guess I am a slow learner.

Too Close for Comfort

GARY AND I had been great friends since we graduated from Bloomington High School way back in 1958.

We also had a close relationship with two other buddies, Bud Pavey and Robert Stanton.

Gary and I spent the next six years chasing girls, roller skating, bowling, and attending every Indiana University basketball game we could.

In 1964, I got married to Kay, and when Gary got out of the army a couple of years later, he robbed the cradle and married Marylin.

Pretty soon children came into the picture; Jeffery and Amber joined the Gross family, and Dawn, Kimberly, and Kevin joined the Goodmans. After that, we were set to do many things for the next forty years. There were cookouts, camping trips, birthday celebrations, and, of course, IU basketball games.

When the kids were young, they loved to go to IU basketball games to pick up the plastic Hoosier souvenir drinking cups. After a game was over, we sometimes left Assembly Hall with fifty or sixty cups. (I just hope the people were done with them before the kids collected them.)

In 1975, we had an opportunity to take a vacation together. Kay's sister had moved to Wauchula, Florida, a year earlier and had invited the two families to come down for a visit. Kay's parents lived next door, so there would be room for all of us.

The kids' school districts had spring break at the same time, the last two weeks of March, so it cleared the way for all of us to make the long drive south.

But I had a big problem: I had the good sense to purchase a Pinto as the family car (it was later called one of the worst cars ever made), and I sure didn't want to make a two-thousand-mile round trip to Florida in a Pinto.

Gary had a big and roomy Chevy Impala, and he suggested we all ride together in his car.

I said, "Gary, do you really think we could all ride in one car?" After all, there were eight of us (Kevin had not been born yet) and lots of luggage.

"Sure," he said. "No problem."

While I admired Gary's optimism, I had my reservations about the whole operation—as it turns out, with good reason.

So, believe it or not, all eight of us (four adults and four children between ages four and nine), piled into the two-door Chevy and headed to Florida. Some of the kids had to sit on whoever's lap was available; others had to squeeze in between the adults.

Four kids and four adults makes eight bladders, which made for a lot of pit stops along the way to Florida. We arrived in pretty good shape, considering everything.

That Saturday, an event happened that almost ruined the whole vacation for me: Indiana lost to the Kentucky Wildcats and was eliminated from the NCAA basketball tournament, which they were favored to win. But the thought of lounging on a sandy beach in Florida brought my spirits up.

I worked at the Spencer Post Office and had left our hosts'

address in Florida with them. Two days later, I got a condolence card with a message of sympathy because of the death of IU's basketball-title dreams. It was signed by all the employees (except the one Purdue fan) and sent by the assistant postmaster, Art Childress—funny guy, that Art.

We were near the beautiful beaches of Sarasota, so we spent every day on those beaches and under lots and lots of sunshine. We had a great time until the night we were to return home.

As snowbirds from Indiana, we failed to put on enough sunscreen for our week in the Florida sun. All eight of us had varying degrees of sunburn! As we headed off for the two-day journey home, I heard, "Oh, ouch, don't touch me." That old saying "too close for comfort" had real meaning for the next miserable one thousand miles.

At the beach: Kim, Amber, Kay, Marylin, Dawn, and Jeff.

Marylin's Revenge

THE ATTACK WAS unexpected, as Gary and I were playing a two-handed card game.

Marylin had snuck up behind me and plopped a gooey mess on top of my head. I wasn't too worried, because I thought it was Play-Doh. It turned out to be Silly Putty.

The difference? Play-Doh is easily removed. It is almost impossible to get Silly Putty out of your hair, as I soon found out.

Everyone took a turn at trying to remove the goo, but as much hair came out as did the putty.

I think this attack was revenge for the rubber snake I had put in Marylin's sleeping bag one time the two families had gone camping.

I admit, I probably deserved some payback for the rubber snake. However, years later I really outdid myself in the prank department. On Marylin's birthday, I placed a personal ad in the Bloomington *Herald-Times* wishing her a happy fortieth birthday. The only problem was she was just turning thirty-five years old. That week, many of her church members wished her a happy fortieth birthday.

She has had thirty years to think of a get-even trick.
I am not looking forward to it.

Marylin is posing with me on my Yamaha
motorcycle—but no way would she ride on it.

Pooch in a Pouch

DAD DIED IN 1971 after a long battle with lung cancer. He spent the last few weeks of his life at home, bedridden. So I didn't blame Mother for not wanting to stay in that house alone.

Because they were only renting, it was an easy decision to pack up and move elsewhere.

I worked at the Spencer Post Office, delivering letters to all parts of town, so I knew where to find an apartment. I found Mother a nice three-bedroom apartment.

Mrs. Hendershot lived in the main house and rented out the apartment; she said it was okay for Mother to keep her Chihuahua, named Cricket. One afternoon, I was nearing the end of my route on Harrison Street when I saw Cricket running loose. She was about four blocks from her new home.

I picked the dog up and put her in my mailbag, as it was now empty, and headed back to the post office to turn in my collected mail before bringing Cricket back to Mother.

The post office shared an alley with the *Spencer Evening World*, the town newspaper. Tom Douglas, who worked for the paper, spotted me and asked if he could take a picture to put in the newspaper. His caption read, "Pooch in a Pouch."

This is me giving Cricket a ride at the end of my mail route. The irony of the picture is that hanging on my mailbag is a can of dog-repellent spray.

The Only Good Snake
Is a Dead Snake

IN 1984, MY wife, Kay, and I owned and operated a pizza café at 201 W. Morgan Street in Spencer.

Kay ran operations, and I made deliveries. One of our daily customers was a local caricature by the name of Randall "Cowboy" Hatton. He was called Cowboy because he always wore a cowboy hat and boots.

Our seven-year-old son Kevin loved to hear him tell stories about the Old West. Kevin would hang on every word.

One summer day when Kevin and I were outside in our yard, Kevin spotted a small garter snake near our front step. Kevin managed to capture the snake and put it in a shoebox. It was to be his pet.

"I want to go to the pizza shop and show Cowboy my pet snake," he said.

Rushing up to the table where Cowboy was sitting, Kevin shouted, "Cowboy, look what I got!" Cowboy looked in the shoebox. He took the garter snake out of the box by its tail. He then cracked the small snake like a bullwhip, breaking its neck and killing it instantly.

Cowboy put the dead snake back in the show box. He then told a shocked Kevin, who had tears in his eyes, "Remember, Kevin, the only good snake is a dead snake."

Kevin with his friend Randall "Cowboy" Hatton.

Kim, as a teenager, often worked behind the counter.

Kay in the kitchen.

Yep, He Needs to See a Specialist

WHEN KEVIN WAS ten years old, he started taking judo lessons at the Monroe Country YMCA.

The class was one hour long, and with the exercises and workouts, it was a tough hour.

I would watch the workouts. Then one day Kevin said I should take the class too, and I agreed to do so. I had to do my workouts with John Hampton, the judo instructor.

John also taught judo at IU, and one time one of his college students attended the class.

He was a purple-belt rank, but because he was about the same size as me, we were paired for our mock fights.

The drill we did was the one where your opponent grabs your shirt and, while sweeping your right foot, throws you on your back for a pin.

But I made a bad mistake and tried to avoid the sweep by stepping back with my left leg. When my opponent threw me down on my back, my left leg was doubled back under me. It snapped my anterior cruciate ligament (ACL).

The ACL injury is the one that puts the football and basketball players out of action for at least a year.

I went to the ER at the hospital, but the doctor said my knee was so swollen that they couldn't do anything for it.

He told me I needed to see an orthopedic specialist. So when another doctor passed by, the doctor examining me stopped him and said, "Look at this knee, I say he needs to see a specialist. What do you think?"

The other doctor glanced down at my knee for maybe five seconds and said, "Yep, he needs to see a specialist."

When I got my bill for the ER visit, the doctor who said, "Yep, he needs to see a specialist," had billed my insurance company for seventy-five dollars, as a "consultation" fee.

Kevin and I in martial arts judo wear. Kevin was in many tournaments in his three years of judo. I worked out for six weeks and was maimed.

The Devil Made Me Do It

FOR YEARS KAY had operated a "haunted house" at the fairgrounds for charity. The large building was always divided into seven rooms with all sorts of displays designed to scare you. Most were pretty elaborate, like an operating room where four or five "doctors" would be removing all sorts of "body parts" from an unlucky patient, to a phony train bearing down on you with really good sound effects.

One year I planned a really simple display in my small room. I would be dressed as the devil, with a full face mask, gloves, and a rubber pitchfork. I set up a wooden support that I would lean on and placed cheap-looking cardboard flames at the base. I had a phony electrical cord running from my back to an overhead light, giving the impression that the devil's eyes might light up or emit "scary sounds".

They started letting people in, so I took my pose. Two girls, about twenty years old, came flying in, screaming from what they had already seen. The girl who was the most shook up flopped at the base of my exhibit, still shaking. Her friend told her, "Get up, and let's finish this." "No," she said. "I am not going back out there. Everything looks so real." Even this fake dummy looks real."

I raised my pitchfork and bellowed, "Who are you calling fake?" She scrambled for the door, screaming all the way. She lost a shoe, which she picked up and threw at me. She never came back for it.

Dressed as the devil at work at the Spencer Post Office, circa 1994.

Part of the Brotherhood

WHILE DELIVERING MAIL on East Franklin Street one day, I saw a motor scooter and a 125cc motorbike for sale. They looked to be in good condition and were only for sale because the two kids who had ridden them had gotten new ones.

I bought them for Kim and Dawn to ride around the neighborhood.

The one I bought for Dawn was the 125cc motorbike, made by Harley-Davidson. It was the smallest motorcycle ever made.

The bike was just right for Dawn, who was fourteen years old at the time, but I rode it often because it was fun to operate. Although I was too big for it, I sometimes rode it to work.

One day I was riding the little motorcycle back home after work. I stopped for a red light on Morgan Street, which is also Highway 46, 67, and 231.

Just then four Harley "choppers" also pulled up at the stoplight, two next to me and two behind them.

The rider next to me was one scary-looking dude. He weighed about three hundred pounds, wore a German helmet with a spike on top, and wore mirrored sunglasses. And he was staring at me.

I just knew that when the light changed the biker man would kick me and the motorbike over and ride away laughing.

Then the light turned green.

The Harleys roared away, but not before the biker man looked over at me and gave me a thumbs-up.

Thank God I was riding a Harley-Davidson and not a Honda.

This is Dawn on her little Harley. Kim is on her motor scooter.
In the picture it appears that Kim has just had a bright
idea; sadly, it is only the reflection of the flashbulb.

Hey, Mister, You're Going
the Wrong Way

When Kim and I went to Chicago to run in the Chicago Marathon in 2000, we arrived just at the start of the race and had no time to look for the few porta-potties scattered around the starting line. So, when we spotted a few a couple of miles into the race, we knew we had better make a stop when we had the chance.

As we started back into the race, I checked my pocket for my car keys. They weren't there. I must have dropped them at the porta-potty. Fortunately, we had only run about six blocks, so I turned around and headed back to find my keys. While I was running at the edge of the street, against thousands of runners, a young voice from the sidewalk hollered out, "Hey, mister, you're going the wrong way!"

The LaSalle Bank Chicago Marathon
October 24, 1999

Donald Goodman   5:10:06

Chip Time 5:10:06   Pace Per Mile 11:49.6
You Placed 21840th of 24687 Total Finishers

We present this certificate to you in honor of your successfully completing
the 1999 LaSalle Bank Chicago Marathon.
Through months of dedicated training and outstanding effort,
you reached for the best within yourself and finished 26 miles and 385 yards.
Congratulations from the people of the City of Chicago and LaSalle Bank.

Norman Bobins
President and Chief Executive Officer
LaSalle Bank N.A.

Richard M. Daley
Mayor
City of Chicago

Corey A. Pinkowski
Executive Race Director
The LaSalle Bank Chicago Marathon

This certificate states that I ran the Chicago Marathon in 5:10:06. That slow time would suggest that I ran the "wrong way" longer than I thought.

Easy—I Cheated

THE BOSTON MARATHON is the most prestigious race in the country. You must qualify for it by running a fast time based on your age. And this must be done in a sanctioned marathon before you are invited to run.

They only want elite runners, who are serious about running. If this is the case, how did I, one of the slowest runners on the planet, get an invitation to run Boston? Easy—I cheated.

I didn't aim to, but I did.

It began when Dawn asked Kim and I to run with her in the Country Music Marathon in Nashville in the spring of 2002.

Dawn and Kim were signed up to do the half marathon (13.1 miles), and I was registered in the full (26.2 miles). The two races are run together at the same time. The three of us ran together, and as we neared the end of the half marathon, it started to rain.

I didn't want to run in the rain by myself, so I crossed the finish line with Kim and Dawn. The finish line was at the NFL Tennessee Titan Stadium.

Our times were officially recorded using a chip we wore on our shoes.

Because I paid the fee for the full marathon, my time was recorded as such, making me eligible to run Boston, by mistake.

This is the Country Music Half Marathon. Dawn, Kim, and I crossed the finish line together.

This certificate shows my time in the Country Music Marathon as 2:20:51; that qualified me for the Boston Marathon. In fact, it was a poor time for even a half marathon.

Don Goes Ape

WHEN I WAS working at the post office, most of the time I would arrive at about 6:15 a.m. so I could unload the mail truck that came in at 6:30 a.m. Dan Wampler, who was the janitor, would also usually come in at 6:15 a.m. to turn on the coffeemaker.

One winter morning when it was still dark, I parked over on Harrison Street and arrived early at 6:00 a.m. I was carrying a full gorilla suit that Kay used at the haunted house.

I put on the gorilla suit, locked the door again, and turned off the lights. I waited for Wampler to come into the break room. When he did, I jumped out of the darkness and let out a big growl. Wampler threw up his hands and staggered backward as I doubled over in laughter.

Looking back on this episode, I now question the wisdom of me jumping out of the darkness in a gorilla suit at a middle-aged man who was seventy-five pounds overweight.

What if he had been carrying a weapon? And how would I explain to the police if he had died of fright—that I was just an innocent bystander in a gorilla suit?

I and two of my coworkers at my open-house retirement in September 2005. Gary Cummings is on my right, and Dan Wampler is on my left.

If you take notice of the size of Gary Cummings, you'll know why I didn't play my childish prank on him instead of Dan.

Mark Greene in the famous gorilla suit. With him is his handsome trainer, Momar.

Ten More Feet and I Would Have Made the Runway

ONE DAY I heard a low-flying aircraft of some kind approaching overhead. It was a strange-looking machine. It looked like a three-wheel go-cart hanging from a fifty-foot-wide parachute.

It was going about twenty-five miles per hour and was about three hundred feet in the air.

I found out later that it was called an ultralight. It was classified as an experimental aircraft and as such didn't require a license to fly.

There are two kinds of ultralights. One is a fixed-wing, like a regular airplane, and the other is a powered parachute, like the one I saw.

I found out where the pilot lived and paid him a visit. He lived on a farm and used one of his fields as a landing strip.

I asked him if he would teach me to fly his powered parachute. He said that he would for twenty-five dollars. But first I needed to sign a waiver absolving him of any blame if I died during the flying lesson.

Already this was sounding like fun. My flying lesson consisted of flying around Spencer for about forty-five minutes, with two takeoffs and landings from the tiny field behind his barn.

I was to have my solo flight the next morning at 6:00 a.m. We were going to use the 2,300-foot grass runway at Shawnee Airport, near Bloomfield.

My instructor explained that it was better for me to solo on the long grass runway at Shawnee rather than on the field behind his barn that sometimes had cows and sheep in it.

During my solo flight, I lifted off fairly smoothly, climbed to an altitude of three hundred feet, and leveled off. I circled the airport for about thirty minutes. Then my instructor, by two-way radio, told me it was time for my first landing.

He said I should sit the plane down about halfway down the runway for a good smooth landing. I dropped to about ninety feet and headed straight for the runway. My plan was that at about seventy-five yards out I would cut power, dropping to about fifteen feet above ground, then increase power to fly halfway down the runway, and then land.

I didn't know that there was a three- or four-second delay in getting power to the motor. So when I got down to about seventy-five feet from the ground, I gave it some gas to halt the descent at fifteen feet. That didn't really happen until I touched down and rolled to a stop, ten feet from the 2,300-foot runway that airplanes are supposed to use for landings.

Me and my flying machine. In the background is the 2,300-foot-long grass runway that I landed on … 10 feet short.

I flew this for eight years before selling it in 2010.

Kim's Ironman Triathlon

EARLY THIS YEAR I found an old birthday card from Kim, and she had written a personal note with it, here it is word for word:

Happy Birthday!

> *Some of my best father-daughter memories are imbedded in our running adventures. There was the first marathon where you left your keys in your jacket in the porta-potty!*

> *The Air Force marathon in Dayton, your ankle was so swollen from the lawn mower incident, that you took six Aleves before the race.*

> *The Towpath marathon in Cleveland, your feet got so bloody and blistered that you drove home barefoot. Then, after the Columbus marathon, we walked around for two hours trying to find our hotel.*

> *The half marathon in Nashville, Tennessee with Sue, you suggested the gas stations as a possible pre-race dinner venue.*

> *My very favorite memory, though, is you running the last 4 miles of my first Ironman with me. I was so tired.*

*It was already dark. I heard your keys jangling in
your pocket first, hen noticed your glow-stick necklace.
It was a great "moment".*

Love you!

Kim

An Ironman triathlon consists of a 2.4 mile swim, a 112 mile bicycle ride, and a marathon 26.2 mile run, raced in that order without a break. Most Ironman events have a strict time limit of 17 hours to complete a race.

The Ironman race starts at 7:00AM, the mandatory swim cut off for the 2.4 mile swim is two hours and 20 minutes, the bike cut off time is 5:30PM, and all finishers must complete their marathon by midnight.

Kim ran her Ironman in 2006. It was in Northern California, and Kay and I flew out to help encourage her in the race.

The race started in Guerneville, CA, a small town about 100 miles north of San Francisco. That's where we stayed for a week. The Russian River in Guerneville was the site of the swim at 7:00AM. After the swim Kim got on her bicycle to do the bike ride through beautiful Napa Valley countryside, in temperatures reaching into the 90's. The last leg of the race was the marathon that would end in Windsor, CA many hours later.

About 9:00PM Kay and I, along with two of Kim's, Alix and Zoey, positioned ourselves at the start-finish line in Windsor; a city about 30 miles away. So many of the original contestants had dropped out of the triathlon that only a very few were crossing the finish line. I got worried about Kim, so I started running out the race route to find her.

About four miles out I saw her, exhausted from 15 hours of punishment, but still running. I told her how close she was and I would run with her to pick up her spirits.

Now I had not done any running since my colon-cancer operation, the year before, so after running four miles out to greet her, I didn't know if I could run four more miles back to town. But with the slowed down pace we were doing, I knew I could jog with her and she would finish the Ironman triathlon.

When I knew we were only four blocks from the finish line, I went to the side-walk, so she could finish the race by herself.

And she did to cheers of her family and spectators at the finish line.

While in Northern California I rented a bike and
toured the beautiful Napa Valley countryside